Roger the rat tries to discover what his talent might be through trial and error. Is he a nurse? A chef? A barber? After an encounter with a curious cat and a hunt for a missing snake, Roger realizes that his talent may have been hiding under his nose all along.

The Tale of a Talented Rat

By
J.M. Simpson

Illustrated by
Marija Stoisavlevic

For further information contact:
Institute of Reading Development
5 Commercial Blvd.
Novato, CA 94949
www.readingprograms.org

First Edition
Printed in the United States of America

Contents

1

The Untalented Rat

Roger the rat lived with his parents in a cozy nest behind the water heater. The heater warmed the farm house of a human family named the Johnsons. Roger knew that there were three Johnsons: Mr. Johnson, Mrs. Johnson, and Eric Johnson. The rats didn't worry much about the Johnsons. The big folk lived on the other side of rat walls. The Johnsons hardly ever saw the rats. This was for two reasons.

First, rats are quick at hiding. Second, the rats lived in places where humans don't go. Some lived under the floors. Some lived between the walls. Some lived in the attic. Roger could travel all the way to his school in the barn without ever seeing a human. He did this by using the gopher tunnels outside. Most rats could not remember the path through the gopher tunnels. Roger could. He was good at remembering.

Gophers and rats were just some of the animals that lived on the farm. There were also mice, chipmunks, and squirrels. There was a white snake named Cecil. Cecil was Eric Johnson's pet. And then there was the cat.

Marmalade was a furry orange beast with razor claws and glowing eyes. She hunted rodents. One mouse said that the cat laughed

when she ate an animal. All the rodents feared Marmalade.

Even though the rats had to watch for Marmalade, Roger liked his home. He was the smallest in his family. He also had a big brother and sister. His sister had a beautiful voice. Everyone said that her talent had been clear from a young age.

Roger wondered what they meant. He knew clear meant see-through. He tried looking at Amy in the sun. No luck. He still didn't see her talent. He hoped his talent was green.

At school, teachers talked to the rats about finding their place in the world. His friends shared how they would use their talents when they grew up. For example, Serena had the talent of dancing, so she was going to be a ballerina. Martin said he was going to study plants.

Roger didn't have a talent, as far as he could tell. He decided to start looking for one. He was very good at finding things. So Roger hunted. He found lost coins. He found rubber bands. But he didn't find a talent.

Maybe I could find my talent if I knew its shape, Roger thought.

"Is my talent round?" he asked his mom.

She smiled at him. "A talent is something you are good at doing, Roger," she explained.

"For example, my talent is nursing."

"Do you think nursing is my talent too?" Roger asked.

She told him that he could visit the hospital and find out.

Roger woke up early on the day of the hospital visit. His tummy felt full of wiggly worms. Maybe that is how it felt when your talent was growing. At the hospital, he watched his mom write down numbers on charts. He remembered each number. Maybe he would be good at nursing. Then he watched her pull out a needle for a shot. His tummy felt very, very wiggly. And he felt dizzy. When a drop of blood came out of the mouse's paw, Roger sank to the floor. Nursing was not, not, NOT his talent.

So Roger tried doing a lot of other things. He spent a week with Grandad Tim. Grandad built tables and chairs for rats. But after

Roger chatted all morning and hammered his finger, Grandad sent him home.

His brother Matt was a talented chef at the rat restaurant in the greenhouse. Maybe Roger should be a chef too. So Roger joined Matt for a day. The morning passed happily. Roger liked working in the kitchen.

He studied the cookbook. He understood everything about stew. Well, except for the last bit. The book said to add a dash of pepper. Roger blinked. He knew that dash meant "hurry" or "run." Some rats ran races called the hundred-yard dash.

Maybe a dash of pepper meant that he had to toss pepper in the stew while running past the pot. That sounded fun. Matt had never said that he had to run around the kitchen while cooking! He looked for his brother. Matt was busy on the phone. So Roger picked up the open jar of pepper and backed up to the door. That gave him lots of room to run.

As he dashed past the stove, he tossed the whole jar of pepper into the pot.

All went well until some squirrels ate the stew. They started coughing.

"Too much pepper!" cried one squirrel between spasms.

"Roger, what did you do?" cried his brother.

Roger explained.

Matt sighed. "When you are cooking, a dash of something means 'just a little bit,'" he said.

Roger's dad comforted him that night. "Cooking is not your talent, son," he said. "But you'll figure it out. Some rats need more time than others."

Roger thought his dad was right. He went out and bought five watches. Surely with five watches, he would have enough time to find his talent.

Yet the days ticked past and Roger was no closer to finding his talent. His birthday came. Roger still did not have a talent. School ended. Roger's teachers said things like, "Roger is a helpful rat. He tries really hard." But none of them said that he was talented. Roger felt sad.

Finally, Grandad Tim suggested that Roger work in the barbershop for the summer.

"He can learn to trim whiskers and brush fur," said Grandad. "No talent needed."

So it was agreed that Roger would start his first job on Monday.

2

Roger's First Job

The barbershop was under the Johnsons' porch. It was cool and shady. The sweet smell of honeysuckle drifted down from the porch above. The barbershop was popular with all of the rodents. Even large ones came to get their fur done.

Roger was excited about spending time in the barbershop. Animals gathered there to talk. And Roger liked to listen. In fact, he was so excited that he couldn't wait for Monday. So once his room was tidy, Roger set out for the barbershop.

"Hello, everyone," he called. "Roger the rat here."

The barber looked up from shampooing a chipmunk. His whiskers sagged.

"Roger, you are not supposed to start until Monday," he explained. "This is Friday."

"Oh, I know," said Roger happily. "I want to start early."

"I'm very busy today," grumbled the barber. "I don't have time to hold your hand."

Roger thought that was a strange thing to say. No matter how nice the barber was, Roger didn't want to hold his hand. Especially when it was covered in shampoo.

The barber looked at the chipmunk. He looked at Roger.

Roger waited.

"Fine. You can stay," said the barber. "Try not to get in the way."

There were seven animals waiting. Roger sat down to watch. He had to move a notebook off his seat, so he put it in an empty sink. There was nowhere else for it to go.

The barber poured red dye in a bowl and started putting it on the chipmunk's fur.

"Roger," said the barber, "since you are here, please help Mr. Nut to a seat."

Mr. Nut was an old squirrel with bushy white ears. Roger jumped up to help. He held out his arm so the old squirrel could lean on him.

"Who are you?" yawned Mr. Nut.

"Roger. Roger the rat."

"You are not fat at all, young rat," said Mr. Nut.

"No, Mr. Nut," yelled Roger. "I said 'rat,' not 'fat.'"

The squirrel sank onto the seat. "There is no need to shout," he told Roger. "I am not deaf. All I need is an ear trim."

"Roger," said his boss, "please start by brushing his ears."

Roger picked up the brush and got started. He wasn't thinking about brushing. He was thinking about not being able to hear.

14

If people can't hear, they can learn to talk with their fingers. It is called sign language. It might take time for Mr. Nut to learn. He might need a teacher. Maybe Roger could find him a book to learn sign language.

"Roger!" called the barber. "Focus. I need you to trim his ears. Have you ever used clippers before?"

"Yes!" said Roger. He had helped Uncle Monty clip the grass once.

"Good," said the barber. "I didn't know you had worked with clippers. Take off one inch of fur."

Roger laid down the brush. He looked for grass clippers. He did not see any. Instead, he saw a shiny tool on the table. The handle said "Buzz No-Fuzz."

He picked up the tool and turned it on. The buzzing tickled his paw. He looked at Mr. Nut. The old squirrel had closed his eyes. Roger closed his eyes too. It was much easier to focus with closed eyes. Now he couldn't see shiny tools or other rats. Roger relaxed. He thought about Mr. Nut learning to talk with his fingers.

Maybe Mr. Nut should learn to read lips too. Roger could help with that. He could practice talking slowly with Mr. Nut. That way, the squirrel could read his lips. How happy Mr. Nut would be to understand other rodents again! He might even thank Roger for all the help.

"Roger!" yelled the barber.

Roger's eyes flew open. Mr. Nut had no fur left on one ear. The other ear had three tufts sticking up.

"Oops!" said Roger.

Gasps filled the room. Six surprised customers watched.

"My ears!" screeched Mr. Nut. Both of his eyes were wide open now. They glared at Roger.

"Young rat," cried Mr. Nut, "You are the worst barber I have ever seen."

He climbed out of his chair. Roger froze. Mr. Nut shook his paw at Roger. Then he stomped out the door. It slammed after him.

Roger felt cold and then hot.

"Roger, maybe you should stop for the day," said the barber.

"First let me help you clean up," said Roger. He hurried to pick up the bowl of red dye. He dumped it in the sink.

The barber told the chipmunk to pay him at the desk. "Let me get your bill," said the barber. He looked all around.

"Where is the account book?" he asked.

"Account book?" said Roger.

"Yes," said the barber. "I have a notebook where I write down what each customer needs to pay. I was sure I left it on a seat."

Roger felt a cold prickle zoom all the way

from his head to his tail.

"I may have moved that book," he mumbled. "Into the sink. For space."

The barber raced over to the sink. He gave a squeal.

In his paw was a soggy notebook dripping red drops. For a moment, the barber looked like he was going to cry.

"Roger," he said. He spoke as if each word were hard to say. "Wait for me in the back. Don't. Touch. Anything. Else."

3

Marmalade

Roger's day had slipped from good to bad. It had been thirty long minutes since the barber had fired him. The barber said that Roger was not cut out to work in the barbershop. He had listed four big mistakes that Roger had made.

1. Roger was careless.
2. He got distracted.
3. He didn't follow instructions.
4. He didn't ask for help.

Roger paused for a breath. He had not stopped running since he left. The barber's angry words seemed even louder when he slowed down. And he felt worse.

He remembered what Grandad Tim had said. "He can learn to trim whiskers and brush fur. No talent needed."

How wrong Grandad was! It took a lot of talent to be a good barber. That's what the barber had told him.

Roger could not run anymore. His legs shook. Maybe if he drank some water he would feel better.

There was a tiny creek in the woods. He headed towards it. He needed a cool, clear drink of water. Instead he found that someone had tramped through the creek. The water was a muddy brown. There were deep boot prints in the soft dirt. This was the WORST day ever.

If he wanted clean water, he would have to find the water bucket in the barn now. He sighed. He dragged his tail to the barn. After a long drink, he splashed cold water on his hot face and ears. Then he climbed up to the loft. Now he stood on the highest rafter in the barn. Sunset stained the sky pink and red.

He dashed a paw across his eyes. What a bad day! He jumped off a rafter onto a hay bale. What should he do next?

He didn't want to go home and tell his parents. They would feel sad too.

He jumped from the hay to the floor. That's when he knew something was wrong. Instead of landing on wood, his feet hit something soft. Something warm.

Something that said, "Ooof."

Roger had jumped right onto Marmalade!

For a second Roger's heart stopped. Then it hammered in his chest so hard that it shook him. He tried to run, but the cat curled a paw around Roger and held him.

This was the end! He was dead! He was going to be cat food!

A tiny squeak came out of Roger's throat. Then he went limp.

The cat peered at him. Her big green eyes glowed in the dark loft.

"Why are you in the barn?" she asked Roger. "Aren't you a house rat?"

Roger blinked.

"Ummm," he stuttered. "I'm…I'm…"

"In trouble?" asked the cat.

"Yyyyes."

"And alone?"

"Yes."

"And scared," ended the cat.

Roger licked his dry lips. "Please," he whispered. "Please eat me quickly."

"Eat you?" said the cat. She sounded shocked. "Why would I want to eat you?"

"Don't you eat rats?"

"Ugh! No!" said the cat. She opened her paw so that Roger was free. "I'm a pescatarian."

"What's that?"

"I only eat fish," explained the cat. "Or sometimes drink milk. Eat rats? Blah!"

Roger couldn't think of anything to say. He had never felt so surprised.

"But don't you…hunt rodents?" he asked.

"Oh, I have to look busy when the Johnsons are watching," Marmalade agreed. "They are my people. They want me to catch pests. But I never hurt any animals. That would be mean."

"Oh," said Roger. He couldn't think of anything else to say.

"So why are you in trouble?" asked the

cat. She sat up. Her tail curled over her snowy paws.

"I just lost my job," said Roger sadly. "And I don't have any talents."

"Both of those problems can be fixed, can't they?" asked the cat.

Roger sighed. "Not if you are me."

"Well, if I can't help you, maybe you can help me. I have a problem."

Roger felt curious. He was about to find out what kind of problems a cat might have.

4

Missing Snake

"I'm looking for a missing snake," Marmalade told Roger. "The Johnsons' pet snake is named Cecil. He got out of his cage. Again. No one can find him. Eric is very unhappy about it. He has been crying all day. I want to make Eric smile again. Have you seen a snake?"

Roger thought.

"I know the snake you mean," he said. "I

haven't seen him today. But I'm very good at finding things. Maybe I can help you find him."

"That would be most helpful. Where do you suggest we begin?"

It felt good to be helpful. Roger's mind went to work. "Where has Cecil been found before?"

The cat shrugged. "A lot of places. In the air vent. Under the bed. Behind the dryer."

"And have you looked in all those places?"

"Yes. No snake."

"Hmm," said Roger. "What do all those places have in common?"

The cat licked her paw. "I don't know."

"I do!" said Roger. "Behind the dryer is warm. Under the bed is warm. Inside the vent is warm. They are all warm places. Cecil must like warmth."

The cat stopped washing. She stared at

Roger. "I never would have thought of that. Where else is warm?"

Roger thought carefully about it. He pictured all the places in the house. He crossed off all the spots that were cold. Finally, he had three places left.

"Cecil might be near my house," said Roger. "Or he might be under the stove. Or he might be in the attic."

Marmalade jumped up. "Let's go find him. Will you help me look?" Her big green eyes shone with a friendly light. How silly he had been to think the cat looked scary!

"Sure," Roger said.

Marmalade invited Roger to ride on her back.

At the kitchen door she stopped to let Roger off. The Johnsons must not see their cat giving rides to rats. Roger asked the cat to look by the stove. Then they would meet

in the hall near Roger's home.

Roger took the pipes to the water heater. He did not go into his home. He hadn't decided what to tell his family about his bad day.

Instead, he looked for any clue of the missing snake. There were no scale marks in the dust. Nothing had been moved. He heard a meow in the hall. He pushed his way out through a mouse hole near the floor.

At first sight, Roger could tell that the cat had not found the snake. There was a droop to her tail.

"Any luck?" she asked Roger.

"No," said Roger. "There were no prints in the dust. I don't think he has been here at all."

"I heard Mrs. Johnson talking to Eric. She is scared. There have been some break-ins around here lately. Eric now thinks that someone stole his snake."

"Do you think someone stole the snake?"

"No, I'm sure he just got out. Cecil is always getting out of his cage."

Roger looked up and down the hall. "We haven't checked the attic yet," he said. "The attic is the warmest room in the house. Maybe Cecil is there."

"Hop on again," offered Marmalade. "I'll take you up there."

In two quick flicks of a cat's tail, Marmalade and Roger were up the attic stairs. The door to the attic was locked. But Roger knew how to get them inside. He jumped off Marmalade's back and squeezed under the door. Then he climbed up a box. From there he jumped to the door handle. He turned the lock with his paws.

"Now leap against the door," he told Marmalade. "It will bounce open."

Soon both of them were standing in the dim, dusty attic.

"You are very resourceful!" said Marmalade.

"Resourceful?" asked Roger.

"That means you are full of ideas for solving problems."

Roger grinned.

"Now, where would a snake hide in here?" whispered Marmalade.

Roger peered at the floor. Aha! He saw it! There was a thin twisty path in the dust. It led to an old trunk. He pointed it out to Marmalade.

The cat put her nose to the dust and sniffed. She sneezed.

"Issss that the ssssound of my friend Marmalade?" asked a new voice.

"Yes," called the cat.

Her green eyes glowed like lamps in the dark attic. She peered behind the trunk. Roger

followed her. There, in the space between the wall and the trunk, lay the longest white snake that Roger had ever seen.

The snake reared up when it saw them. His scales glittered in the moonlight coming through a skylight.

"Who issss thisss?" asked the snake. He was looking at Roger.

"Cecil, meet my new friend Roger the rat. He's the one who found you."

5

Cecil Gives a Speech

Roger wasn't sure if the white snake liked him. He couldn't tell. He wasn't sure if he liked the snake. The snake looked awfully big. He should have asked Marmalade if the snake ate rodents before they found him.

"I wassssn't lossst," hissed the snake. He started weaving back and forth to coil himself up. "I am running away."

"Not again!" said Marmalade. She sat

down and curled her tail around her snowy paws. "Cecil, how many times have I said it? You can't just run away whenever your cage is left open. Eric loves you. He gets upset when you go missing."

"But my glassss box isss cold," said the snake. "I need warmth."

"And Eric needs you," said Marmalade.

"I have an idea," said Roger. "An idea that will help both Eric and Cecil."

The cat and the snake looked at him.

"Tell ussss," said the snake. He sounded curious.

Roger took a deep breath. His voice was a little squeaky. "You have a problem," he began. "Your cage is too cold, right?"

"Yessss," hissed the snake.

"But when you go out looking for a warmer place, then your boy misses you. If your cage could be warmed up, you would feel a lot better. There is a desk lamp in Eric's room near your cage. Marmalade and I can push your cage under that lamp. That way the lamp can warm your cage and both you and Eric can feel happier."

Marmalade swished her tail in excitement.

"Roger, that's a great idea!" she said. "What do you think, Cecil?"

The snake was staring at Roger. Staring

very hard.

Roger gulped.

"I think," said the snake quietly, "that issss a good idea. Thisss isss a very clever young rat."

Roger smiled. He shook his head. "No, I'm not clever. I don't have any talent."

"What a ssssilly thing to sssay!" said Cecil. "Who told you that you don't have a talent?"

"Everyone."

"Well, I ssssay differently," said the snake. He was all coiled up now, and his head reached the top of the washboard. "I have met hundreds of rodents in my life. And few of them could ssssolve problems. It sssseems that you don't know your own abilities." He drew his neck up importantly.

"Cecil likes to talk," whispered Marmalade. "He's always giving speeches."

Roger sat down politely to listen.

"First, tell me why you agreed to look for me, young rat?" asked Cecil.

Roger thought hard. "Marmalade needed help," said Roger slowly. "And I thought I could help her. I can usually find missing things or animals."

"Sssso," said Cecil. "You like to help others. That's a gift. Now how did you know where to find me?"

"I know! I know!" chimed in the cat. "He asked me where you hid before. Then he told me that all those spots were warm. He thought about other warm spots in the house, and then we checked each one."

"Aha," said the snake. "Roger is curious. He asks lots of questions. And he thinks about what he has learned. All very important skills."

Important for what? Roger wondered.

"Then, young rat, you use deductive thinking to solve problems."

"What's deduc…deductive thinking?" asked Roger.

"It is a logical way of thinking that helps you come up with answers. You noticed that I like warm places and thought about all the warm places in the house."

"You also have a good memory," Cecil added. "You were able to list all the warm places in the house. Finally, you pay attention to what you see and hear. How did you know that I was behind the trunk?" he asked Roger.

"I saw your trail in the dust," explained Roger.

"Good observation skills," said Cecil. "Yes, my young friend, you have the makings of a talented detective."

Roger felt warm from the tip of his tail to his ears. A detective! Him?

"Do you really think so?" he asked.

The cat and the snake both nodded.

"A great private eye," said the cat.

"My eyes aren't really private," said Roger. "And I have two, not just one."

Cecil hissed with laughter. "It is a sssaying," he explained. "It means that you can use your eyes and your skills to find things. Or to solve problems for others."

Roger smiled. "Do you think other animals could use a private eye?"

"Oh, yes!" said Marmalade. "I am always losing my catnip toy. I would pay you to find it."

"And I..." began the snake. But he didn't finish. Before he could say one more word, the animals heard a scream from downstairs.

6

Catching a Burglar

"A rat in my pantry!" screamed Mrs. Johnson. "Marmalade! Marma-LADE!"

The three animals in the attic froze. Marmalade looked at Cecil. Cecil looked at Roger.

"I need to go downstairs," said Marmalade.

"And I should sslither back to Eric's room," said Cecil.

"And I should be..." Roger began.

Suddenly Roger did not know what he should be doing. His happiness slipped away. There was nothing more for a detective rat to do.

Suddenly Mrs. Johnson screamed again. This time her scream was louder.

"Help! Help! We've been robbed!"

"This sssounds sserious," said Cecil.

"Roger, Cecil," said Marmalade, "Please come with me. It sounds like the Johnsons need help."

After some fussing, Cecil agreed to ride on the cat's back in front of Roger.

"Don't let me fall off," Cecil warned. "This cat is ssslippery."

"I won't let you fall," grunted Roger, pushing the heavy snake up on Marmalade's back. He climbed up and gripped the cat's neck with his back legs. He held onto the snake with his front paws. It was hard not to slip. He pretended he was riding a horse.

Marmalade dashed for the living room. They heard a babble of voices.

Marmalade stopped at the door to let Cecil and Roger slide off her back. Roger and the snake hid in the hall and peeked through the doorway, careful to stay out of sight of the humans.

This is what they saw:

Mrs. Johnson was crying on Mr. Johnson's shoulder. She was saying, "Mama's jewelry!

Gone! All gone!"

Mr. Johnson kept saying, "It will be okay, honey. At least none of us were hurt."

Eric stood in the middle of the room. He was staring at the empty space where the television had been. A few wires stuck out of the wall.

Roger looked across the glossy wood floor.

He saw something. There were big, muddy boot prints right by the empty television stand. And another set by the open window.

It was a print he had seen before. His mind went to work. Where had he seen muddy boot prints earlier that day? He remembered! He had seen prints in the mud by the creek. The track in the mud was the same as the track on the Johnsons' floor. That meant that sometime that day, the burglar had crossed the creek in the woods. Maybe he was still in the woods.

Roger's eyes lit up. It was a problem. And he was good at solving problems.

"Cecil," he whispered. "I have an idea. I'll need you and Marmalade. Let's get the cat to come over here and I'll tell you my plan."

It took time for the cat to notice Roger. Marmalade was busy purring and rubbing her head against the Johnsons' legs. Finally she saw Cecil and Roger waving to her. She came over and sat down by them.

"What's up?" she whispered.

Roger thought it was a silly question. Yet he did not want to be rude. So he answered. "Up is the opposite of down."

"No, no, no," said Cecil. "By sssaying, 'what's up,' the cat is asking about your plans."

"Oh, my plans. I think I know where the burglar is hiding."

"Where?"

"I saw the same boot print in the woods by the creek today. I don't know if the man is still there. But it is worth looking. Since Marmalade is the fastest, she should go look."

Roger told the cat where to find the print

in the woods. Marmalade slipped out the cat door. While she was gone, Roger told Cecil the next part of his plan.

"If the burglars are still in the woods, we need to get the Johnsons out there. But the Johnsons will only follow an animal if it has something they want," he said.

Cecil nodded.

"They want you," Roger pointed out. "So if they see me running out with you in my mouth, they will follow us."

"Ick! I'm not going in your mouth!" hissed Cecil.

"Fine! I'll hold you in my paws. Marmalade can meow so they see us at the right time. But I want to do more. I want to scare the burglars back toward the Johnsons," said Roger. "How can animals scare humans?"

Cecil flicked his tongue. "Easy. Humans run away from sssnakes. I am only a pet snake, but Eric's friends are still scared of me."

Roger was thinking about what Cecil had said. He had said "snakes." Plural. More than one snake. If only there were more snakes who could help them.

Cecil was also thinking about snakes. He added, "Now a really scary looking snake is the king snake. Red and yellow stripes. Danger colors. Most people think it is bad. And it is big. Whenever I get out of my cage, I like to visit the den of king snakes behind the house."

"How many are there?"

"About twelve. Or fifteen. One time I said to them—"

Roger did not let him finish. "Do you think they would help us scare away some burglars, Cecil?"

Cecil narrowed his eyes. He did not like

being interrupted.

"Perhaps. If I asked them. As a favor."

There was a thump on the porch.

Marmalade crawled back through the cat door. Her orange fur stood on end with excitement.

"The burglars are still there, Roger! They are counting boxes. But they have a truck loaded with stuff. It looks like they might leave soon."

"Then we need to act now," said Roger. He turned to Cecil. "It is time to ask your friends for that favor."

7

Roger, Detective Rat

By the time the clock chimed eight, Roger's plan was in motion. Cecil had slithered outside to ask the king snakes for their help.

Marmalade had promised to get the Johnsons to look at the kitchen door at 8:15 by meowing loudly. That was when Roger planned to run out the cat door with Cecil. He would head for the woods.

Roger took another glance at the clock. 8:10 already.

Cecil should have come back by now.

A little while ago a policeman had shown up to file a report. The policeman and the Johnsons stood around the kitchen table. The policeman asked questions. Whenever the Johnsons answered, the policeman wrote notes on his report.

Roger chewed his nails. 8:12 pm. Where was the snake?

Just then Mrs. Johnson tripped over Marmalade for the second time. She let out a sputter.

"I can't move without falling over this cat tonight. Eric, go shut her up in the bedroom."

No! thought Roger. Oh, no!

Marmalade leaped for the door. But Eric moved faster. In a second, the boy had the cat in his arms and took the wiggly animal down the hall.

"Bad kitty," he said, as he closed her in a room.

Roger felt a thrill of panic shoot up his spine. Without his friends, his plan was falling apart!

The clock chimed. It was 8:15.

Still no Cecil.

Roger drew in a long breath. He had to stay calm. He had to think. Cecil had told him he was good at thinking. He could solve this problem.

If he couldn't lead the humans outside with Cecil, he would have to find something else that humans wanted. His eye followed the moving pen in the policeman's hand.

And then he knew.

Roger climbed on the kitchen counter. He took a running leap for the table. He landed on three paws and slid across its

smooth surface. He crashed onto the report. Grabbing it in his teeth, he kept going.

Screams filled the room. There was a whoosh of air. Roger felt his fur ruffled by a hand that just missed him. He jumped off the table, still holding the paper in his jaws.

More yelling.

The policeman raised his foot and tried to step on Roger.

But Roger was too fast for him.

He darted left. Then right.

With a burst of speed, he jumped through the cat door. The paper crunched. There was a ripping sound as Roger pushed his way onto the porch.

He heard eight pairs of feet pounding behind him. The humans threw open the kitchen door in time to see Roger race towards the woods.

Would they follow?

Roger turned to see.

Yes, the policeman and Eric were still chasing him.

Mrs. Johnson was yelling on the porch. Mr. Johnson had gone back inside for a flashlight.

Roger ran. He thought about all the times

he had run in a gopher tunnel. He had always been fast. He just had to keep breathing and keep ahead of the humans.

His side hurt. He kept running. He was almost to the woods.

Suddenly there were shouts ahead of him.

Three big men rushed out of the woods. They were running, and yelling, and waving their arms.

The one in front yelled, "Monster snakes!"

The middle one called, "Run faster!"

The one in back blubbered, "I don't care how much you pay me. I'm not getting in the truck with a bunch of snakes crawling in it!"

Roger stopped.

The policeman and Eric stopped.

Mr. Johnson stopped.

They all watched as three men sprinted towards the house. The men kept tripping

and yelling and shoving.

Behind them was one of the strangest sights that Roger had ever seen. It looked like the ground was moving. Rippling.

Then he understood. Snakes were moving over the ground. Brown snakes, green snakes, snakes with stripes. They were all slithering out of the woods towards the burglars, moving together like a wave. At the very front Roger saw a long white snake.

Cecil saw Roger. He flicked his tongue.

"Ssssorry, Roger," he hissed. "My friends begged me to lead them. I couldn't ssssay no."

Roger thought Cecil could have said no. It was easy to say those two letters. He knew right then that Cecil might be talented at making speeches, and talented at scaring burglars, but was very untalented at following orders. However, Roger just smiled. As Roger's dad would say, "All's well that ends well."

Just then Eric saw his snake. "Cecil!" cried Eric. The boy ran towards the white snake and picked him up. "Those bad guys stole you!"

The policeman didn't see the snakes. He and Mr. Johnson were busy arresting the three burglars.

The snakes did not come past the edge of the woods. By the time that the policeman had put the burglars in his car, Cecil was the only snake in sight. The policeman and Mr. Johnson did find the stolen goods. They were in a black truck in the woods.

Roger stayed under a bush. No one remembered the paper he had taken now. He was safe. And tired. Very tired. It seemed like years ago that he had gone to the barbershop. He blinked up at the moon. Suddenly a large fuzzy head with two green eyes appeared between him and the moon.

"Roger?"

"Marmalade?"

"Mrs. Johnson just let me out," said the cat. "I came looking for you. I hear you saved the day."

Roger shook his head. "It is night time."

Marmalade's laugh was soft in her throat. "Saving the day," she told him, "means that you solved all the problems. You helped me find Cecil. You thought of a way to make his cage warmer. Then you came up with the plan to catch the burglars. You helped the Johnsons find their stolen stuff."

"Oh," said Roger.

"Congratulations, Detective Roger," said the cat. "Now would you like a ride home, my friend? You must be tired. A talented rat needs sleep."

Roger smiled. "That's what my parents always say to my sister."

"And now they will say it to you."

"Will I see you again?"

"Of course. I'll be your first customer in line tomorrow."

And she was.

J. M. Simpson is a children's author with a youthful spirit, a lifelong love of literature, and a fondness for tea. She resides in North Carolina, surrounded by old mountains and young children. Her work for the Institute of Reading Development fulfills a dream to help young readers fall in love with books.

Marija Stoisavlevic has been a children's book illustrator, painter, and printmaker for over 16 years. She has a lifelong love of art and design and, above all, is passionate about illustrating children's books. Marija lives in Belgrade, Serbia.